MOTHER GOOSE MONSTERS®

in

THE REAL MONSTER GOOSE

Written by **Naomi Althen**

Illustrated by **Richard Walz**

For Jennifer Lynne—R.N.W.

Acknowledgments: Thanks to the following people for their kind help: Tali Amit, Lauren Ariev, Daniel Gercke, Jennifer Harris, Thea Mohr, Dave Werner, Leah Werner, Margot Werner, Suzanne Werner, and Selma Zuckerman.

There was an old monster who lived in a shoe,
She had so many children she didn't know what to do.
She gave them some soup, without any bread.
She told them all ghost tales and put them to bed.

Monday's child
is scary to meet,

Tuesday's child
has got big feet,

Wednesday's child is
grouchy and gruff,

Thursday's child
thinks he's tough,

Friday's child
can fly away,

Saturday's child
is here to stay.

And the child born
on the seventh day
Is always dancing,
I'm happy to say.

Little Zazu Flinders
Sat among the cinders
Warming her purple little toes.
Her mother came and caught her,
Hugged her little daughter
For soiling her nice, new clothes.

Little Boy Boo,
Come haunt our house.
Creep up the staircase,
Quiet as a mouse.
Where is the beast
With the big, sharp teeth?
He's under my bed now,
Fast asleep.

Here am I,
Little Jumping Moe,
When nobody saw me,
I jumped on my toe!

is is the house that Zack built.

This is the monster
That lives in the house that Zack built.

This is the rat
That ran past the monster
That lives in the house that Zack built.

This is the dog
That frightened the rat
That ran past the monster
That lives in the house that Zack built.

This is the ghost
That worried the dog
That frightened the rat
That ran past the monster
That lives in the house that Zack built.

This is the monster with the crumpled hat
That caught the ghost
That worried the dog
That frightened the rat
That ran past the monster
That lives in the house that Zack built.

This is the monster with the big, fat cat
That's friends with the monster with the crumpled hat
That caught the ghost
That worried the dog
That frightened the rat
That ran past the monster
That lives in the house that Zack built.

This is the spider all creepy and crawly
That snuck by the monster with the big, fat cat
That's friends with the monster with the crumpled hat
That caught the ghost
That worried the dog
That frightened the rat
That ran past the monster
That lives in the house that Zack built.

This is the frog all slithery and slimy
That ate the spider all creepy and crawly
That snuck by the monster with the big, fat cat
That's friends with the monster with the crumpled hat
That caught the ghost
That worried the dog
That frightened the rat
That ran past the monster
That lives in the house that Zack built.

Handy-spandy, Zack-a-dandy,
Loves bug cake and slimy candy.
He bought some at a grocer's shop,
And out he came, hop, hop, hop.

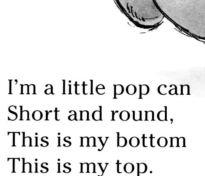

I'm a little pop can
Short and round,
This is my bottom
This is my top.

When you want to drink me,
Pop my top.
But don't try to shake me up!

Ice-cold pops!
Ice-cold pops!
One a dollar, two a dollar,
Ice-cold pops!

Ice-cold pops!
Ice-cold pops!
If you have no vampires,
Give them to some fiends,
Ice-cold pops!

Wiggly wormies hot,
Wiggly wormies cold,
Wiggly wormies in the pot
Nine days old.
Witches like it hot,
Warlocks like it cold,
Monster Goose likes it in the pot
Nine days old.

Baa, baa, black sheep,
Have you any wool?
Yes, Moe, yes, Moe,
Three bags full.

One for Monster Goose,
One for the same,
And one for the boy
I meet in the lane.

The eepy, creepy spider
Lived in the water spout.
Up rose the moon
And called the monsters out.
Out came the sun
And chased the ghouls away,
And the eepy, creepy spider
Slept in the spout all day.

Dragon be nimble,
Dragon be quick,
Dragon breathe fire
To light the candlestick.

Zazu Hall,
She was so small,
A rat could eat her,
Hat and all!

Mary had a little ghost
Its coat was white as snow,
And every time the lights went out
The ghost began to glow.

It followed her to school one day
Which was against the rules.
It made the monsters laugh and play
To see a ghost at school.

And so the teacher turned it out,
But still it floated near
And waited patiently about
'til Mary did appear.

Why does the ghost haunt Mary so?
The little monsters cry.
Why, Mary spooks the ghost you know,
The teacher did reply.

Hick-a-more, Hack-a-more,
On the teacher's classroom door,
All of the monsters,
And all of the ghouls,
Couldn't drive Hick-a-more, Hack-a-more,
Off the teacher's classroom door.

I do not like you, clanging bell,
The reason why I cannot tell.
But this I know, and know full well,
I do not like you, clanging bell!

Goria, Goria, peaches and cream,
Kissed the boys and made them scream.
When the girls came out to play,
Goria, Goria, ran away.

Ring-a-ring-roses,
Step on monsters' toeses,
Witches, Warlocks,
They all fall down!

Giggle, Wiggle, Monster Moe,
How we wonder where you go.
At the game of hide-and-seek,
You're the one who can't be beat.
Giggle, Wiggle, Monster Moe,
How we wonder where you go.

This little ghoul went to market.
This little ghoul stayed home.
This little ghoul scared Monster.
This little ghoul scared no one.
This little ghoul cried, "Boo! Boo! Boo!"
All the way home!

For the want of a lace, the sneaker was lost;
For the want of the sneaker, the race was lost;
For the want of the race, the championship was lost
For the want of the championship, the title was lost;
And all for the want of a shoelace.

"I went up one pair of stairs."
    "Just like me."
"I went up two pairs of stairs."
    "Just like me."
"I went into a room."
    "Just like me."
"I looked in a mirror."
    "Just like me."
"I saw a monster!"
    "Just like me!"

I saw a truck a-coming,
It was all painted blue;
And, oh! it was all filled
With scary things for you!

There were vampires in the cabin,
And spiders in the back;
The tires were made of stone,
And covered all in goo.

The twenty serious beasties
That rode upon the roof
Were twenty serious beasties,
And not one of them a goof!

The Haunted House is falling down, falling down, falling down,
The Haunted House is falling down, my scary lady.

How shall we build it up again, up again, up again,
How shall we build it up again, my scary lady?

Build it up with wood and nails, wood and nails, wood and nails,
Build it up with wood and nails, my scary lady.

Wood and nails will burn down, will burn down, will burn down,
Wood and nails will burn down, my scary lady.

Build it up with iron and steel, iron and steel, iron and steel,
Build it up with iron and steel, my scary lady.

Iron and steel will rust and break, rust and break, rust and break,
Iron and steel will rust and break, my scary lady.

Build it up with stone so strong, it will last for ages long,
Build it up with stone so strong, my scary lady!

Mary, Mary,
Oh, so scary,
How does your garden grow?
With horns and nails and goblin tails
And little bones all in a row.

Roses are red,
Violets are blue,
Vampires are scary,
And so are you!

Oh, do you know the boogeyman?
    The boogeyman, the boogeyman,
Oh, do you know the boogeyman,
    Who lives on Dreary Lane?

Victor Viper vexed a vat of vicious vermin.
A vat of vicious vermin did Victor Viper vex.

Zack and Moe went up the hill
To fetch a bottle of water;
Zack fell down, and broke his crown,
And Moe came tumbling after.

Humpty Hector sat on a wall,
Humpty Hector had a great fall;
All the Monster Goose doctors
And all of her friends,
Couldn't put Humpty Hector together again.

Three little ghoulies, they lost their booties
And they began to howl,
Oh, Monster Goose, dear, we sadly fear
Our booties we have lost!
What lost your booties, you naughty ghoulies,
Then you shall have no treats.
Howl, howl, howl,
No, you shall have no treats.

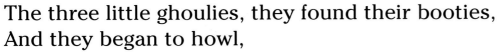

The three little ghoulies, they found their booties,
And they began to howl,
Oh, Monster Goose, dear, see here, see here,
Our booties we have found!
What found your booties, you good little ghoulies,
Then you shall have some treats.
Howl, howl, howl,
Yes, you shall have some treats.

Hey, diddle, diddle!
The ghoul and the fiddle,
The witch jumped over the moon;
The little rat laughed
To see such fun,
And the dish ran away with the spoon.

Three blind bats, see how they fly!
They all swoop down on the monster's wife,
Who scented their cave with sugar and spice.
Did you ever see such a sight in your life
As three blind bats?

Little Miss Muffet
Sat on a tuffet,
Eating her curds and whey;
Along came a spider,
Who sat down beside her,
Took one look and ran straight away.

The Queen of Trolls
She made some rolls
And left them out to harden.
The knave of Trolls
He bowled the rolls
And never asked her pardon.

The King of Trolls,
Did not like the rolls
And really preferred to hide them.
So the knave of Trolls
Kept bowling the rolls
And even got a few strikes in.

Little Boo Hoo
Has lost her shrew
And didn't want to find it.
She left it alone
But it came home
Leaving a mess behind it.

There was a little ghoul, and she had a little curl
Right in the middle of her forehead.
When she was good she scared the whole neighborhood,
When she was bad she was *more* horrid!

Little Moe Tucker
Sings for his supper.
What shall he sing?
A very long song.
But how will he stay up,
all night long?

Little Zack Horner
Sat in a corner
Eating a Halloween pie.
He stuck in his pinky,
Pulled out something stinky,
And said, "What a good ghoul am I."

Pat a cake, pat a cake, monster man,
Make me a monster as fast as you can.
Pat me and paint me, and mark me with a Boo!
And send me trick-or-treating with Moe and Zazu.

Cock-a-doodle-do!
Zazu has lost her shoe.
Hector's lost his guitar pick
And knows not what to do!

Old King Snoal
Was a hairy old troll,
And a hairy old troll was he.
So he picked up the phone
And he dialed with a groan
And he called up his haircutters three.

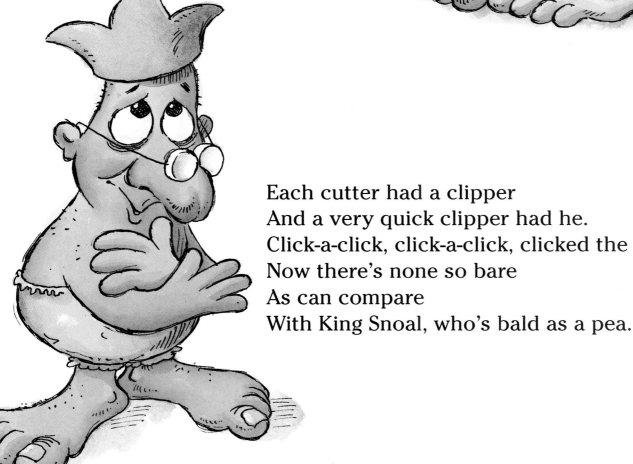

Each cutter had a clipper
And a very quick clipper had he.
Click-a-click, click-a-click, clicked the cutters—
Now there's none so bare
As can compare
With King Snoal, who's bald as a pea.

Peter, Peter, pizza eater,
Had a pet and couldn't keep her.
Put her in a pizza box,
And there he kept his little fox.

There was a scary monster,
And he walked a spooky mile.
He found a ghoulish goblin
And he smiled a creepy smile.
He asked the ghoulish goblin
To come to his haunted house.
And the two lived together
With a sneaky, squeaky mouse.

Vampires, ghoulies, go away,
Come again a rainy day,
Little Monsters want to play.

I had a little monster, the scariest ever seen,
He broke all my dishes and never kept the house clean.
He went to the store to fetch me some flowers,
He didn't come back for over twenty-four hours.
He ate all my bread, he drank all my ale,
He sat by my fire and told me ghost tales.

A was an alligator pie

B burnt it

C carried it

D dropped it

E electrified it

F framed it

G glared at it

H hammered it

I ironed it

J jumped on it

K kidnapped it

L lost it

M mailed it

N napped on it

O outlawed it

WANTED!

REWARD

P pleaded with it

Q queened it

R ran over it

S stared at it

T tied it up

U unzipped it

V vexed it

W weighed it

X, Y, Z all the monsters had fun,
And each monster wanted none.

Monster Goose, Monster Goose, fly away home!
Your house is on fire, your children are gone!

One, two, what shall we do?
Three, four, let's wiggle on the floor.
Five, six, let's give ice cream licks.
Seven, eight, let's slam the gate.
Nine, ten, let's do it again!

Hush, little Monster, don't make a noise,
Mama's going to buy you some creepy toys.
If those creepy toys don't play,
Mama's going to buy you a flying sleigh.
And if that flying sleigh don't go,
Mama's going to buy you a squawking crow.
And if that squawking crow don't caw,
Mama's going to buy you a candy store.
And if that candy store isn't sweet,
Mama's going to buy you some other treats.

Diddle, diddle, dumpling, my monster John
Went to bed with his costume on.
One shoe off, one shoe on,
Diddle, diddle, dumpling, my monster John.

THE END